EVEN THE GODS ARE

JEALOUS

By

ROGER G. MAINE

Contents

Chapter 1

The Arrival

My name is Adrian, but my name is of no value to anyone, hardly to myself. I'm cold; the wind is cold and unbearable. The wind cuts through me like a knife searing my flesh. I don't know where I am, but I know she's close by: Marian, my only love. She must be near. We were scheduled to arrive at the same coordinate points. God knows where.

The feeling is beginning to leave my feet. I'm growing numb. If only Marian were here, we could warm one another. Where is she? God, it's cold. The numbness is creeping upward. I can't move my toes now. I begin to pace and try to keep the blood circulating in my veins. I really wouldn't mind dying, if only she were here. We would at least go together. Unable to pace any further, I must stop. I know I'm beginning to lose the use of my legs below my knees. What started it all? When did this nightmare begin?

My mind wandered back to a time nearly five years ago when life was seemingly contented. My home was on the Planet Urian.

Marian and I were having a wonderful affair. We were living our respective lives, minding our own business. I was doing some experiments with my "music maker"; nothing earth shaking, just some fooling around.

I was living in my quad room (a four-sided room with ante rooms both up and down). I used the upper ante room for my sleeping quarters and the lower one for my music room. The main quad was for viewing the video tapes and daily broadcasts from Urian proper, the major city where the ruler of this quadrant lives.

You would have liked our ruler Uran. I mean, who wouldn't. He is a god. Not in the angelic sense, but a god none the less. Of course, we all are "gods", but Uran is the master of this quadrant. He has powers beyond imagination; at least beyond my feeble imagination.

I would rise every morning and greet the morning suns, and then do my exercises diligently to keep myself in perfect elastic shape. I'm only a child of 150 years, but still I want to keep fit.

My exercises consisted of running a ten-cylinder distance, which would take me only a quarter of a big ring. The bells ring each time anyone has gone around the cylinder one time.

Marian would usually come over shortly after I finished my exercise and we'd play our music-makers together.

I must explain what a music-maker is. It is a piece of flexible material that is mined on Urian. When it is struck, it creates tones which you can manipulate with your hands. The tones become tangible, almost ethereal. We shape them as we wish until they dissolve, and then we do it again. Sometimes Marian and I would get our melodies entwined, and the results were simply chaotic. We did have such fun.

When we weren't making music, we were making love. We really enjoyed making love; better than the music. Marian had been my love partner since my early childhood at 26 years old.   It seems like such a long time ago.

Mother and Dad had consented to our mating, prior to their leaving for their prospective world at 200 years old. Upon attaining the age of 200 years you were graduated from School, and could then go to any spot in the galaxy to create a world of your own. Of course, it had to be done according to specific laws, which were some of the things to be learned in School. It did seem like it took endless years of living for the full power to become apparent within you; after that, another 50 years were spent finishing the final touches to your skills in manipulating matter.

Most of the School was devoted to mental attitudes and clearing the mind.

No negative factors should be allowed to creep into your mind. If that should happen, you could easily forget that you "are a god" and would be subjected to the elements that surround you; God help you!

During School we spent many hours creating and uncreating things. When we got bored, we'd usually sneak out of class, run to our hideaways and just play, make love, or make music. We were really bored with School. They persistently kept at us to practice, so we'd be good "gods".   Never was there any mention of bad gods, since there was no such thing. All that was required to "be a good god" was to do a good job at whatever you undertook to do.

Our major method of transportation was done by our teleporters. We all had one. We merely dialed our point of arrival, pushed the button and we were there. We were all issued a teleporter when we entered School, and were shown how to use it.

Its limit was just around campus and no further distance. It operated on a crystal type of center, with a lower crystal base. It was easy to use.

For teleportation on a national scale or teleportation across the continents, we used the larger walk-in teleporters. Marian and I would often take time out from School, and travel across the nations or to the other side of the Planet to see what changes had been made. The other Schools around our world were always changing the landscape or the weather for their School practice experiments. This was something that Marian and I both enjoyed doing.

They never told you what your next level of learning would be, or what subject you would be studying. Of course, no one ever spoke about what they were studying to another. You only confide in your mate.

(God, it's cold. Where is she? She should have been here by now.)

Chapter II
The Realization

The intense cold brought me back to the present. I moved about to get the circulation going again. God, it was cold. I couldn't even think of having powers, much less, how to go about using them. When the cold had subsided some, I sat down to ponder the situation and recall again how this all came about.

I remember the day well when I stumbled onto the secret that led to all of my troubles. I had been practicing alone with the music- maker. I started to strike it, stumbled, and missed hitting it. In my mind I had already imagined the frequency that I wanted. When I heard the tone I couldn't believe my ears. The tone wasn't audible to others, but I heard it in my head. This time, instead of changing the sound with my hands, as we had always done, I changed the frequency with my mind. I thought it was strange at first, until I happened on a

frequency which neither I nor Marian
had ever encountered. It was really
out of range for my physical ears; only
audible within my mind.

When I would reach this particular
frequency, I noticed my body began to
tremble, and then the vibration in my
body speeded up. Soon the vibration
was so fast that I couldn't feel my body
trembling, though I was still aware that
it was happening. When the trembling
in my body got to its maximum peak I
became sick to my stomach. The sick
feeling passed quickly. Then I noticed
something incredible. My body had
become invisible. I couldn't see my
body and got really scared. I ran to the
mirror in my room, but wasn't able to
see myself in the reflection. Then I
really got frightened. I thought
perhaps I was dying! That couldn't
happen as there never has been a death
of a god reported.

I immediately thought of Marian. I
discovered that I was by her side, a
good three quarters of a cylinder
distance from where my quad living

quarters were, and now I was visible. I was standing directly behind Marian. She turned around and screamed. I really frightened her. She nearly collapsed in my arms. She said she hadn't heard me come into her room, and that it was too late in the day for games. When she saw how excited I was, she knew something was going on.

`I explained to her just what had happened, but all she could do is laugh at me and tell me that she thought I was trying to put one over on her. I told her that I could hardly believe it myself but that it was true.

It was around that time we both noticed I wasn't wearing any clingers. My feet were bare. No one ever goes anywhere without wearing their clingers. Outside the ground is rough, and we need our clingers to protect our feet. In our quad homes, the structure of the floor is soft and resilient and there is no need for footwear.

We both sat down. The enormity of what I had just done was staggering to both of us. The big question in my mind was whether I could do it again. I was too scared now to try it again. Marian tried to question me about it, but I felt too confused to explain it all to her. I wasn't certain myself what had actually happened. All I knew was that it happened, and then I was here with Marian. Oh God! What has happened to me? Am I a freak or something? Marian calmed me down, and she gave me a spare pair of clingers. Then we walked the three quarters of a cylinder back to my quad.

We spoke very little as we trudged back to the quad. I knew that this was something that I just couldn't shrug off. Little did I know what lay ahead of me. Marion returned to her quad, and I laid down to try to get some sleep. What had happened today was the biggest shock of my life. I tried to give it clear thought, but I couldn't calm myself down sufficiently to think straight. After tossing and turning for some time, I finally managed to sleep.

Chapter III
Experimenting

I woke early and, as soon as I got dressed and washed up a bit, I called Marian on the video and asked her to come over. She said she would be right there. Every moment seemed to be an eternity. I have never been so mentally mixed up in my life. What had occurred we all would consider an impossibility, and yet; I know it did happen.

Marian arrived, and fixed a drink of trium to soothe me. She had a glass too; something that neither of us had ever drank during the morning hours. She asked me to think back and describe everything all over again. I started from the beginning.

I had been fooling around with the music-maker as usual, trying for a new and different set of sounds that would be a break-through in "phonics". I wasn't having much luck, when a sound came to my mind. I decided that the sound I thought of was the one

I wanted. I went to strike the music maker, and I tripped and fell. When I got to my feet, I heard the same sound, but the sound was in my head and not in the room. I thought, perhaps, that I had struck my head on something, but I hadn't. The tone was still in my head. Then through force of habit, I tried manipulating the sound and much to my surprise, it changed its frequency. It ran up and down the scale at my will. I was overwhelmed with this new power. I continued manipulating the sounds until I began to see my physical body fade before my eyes. In the mirror on the wall I could see that my body had totally faded away.

I became frightened, and I thought of Marian. Instantly I appeared in her room. She knew the rest of the story. We were both too emotional by this time to deal with the mystery.

Our feelings for each other were running high by this time, and we began to fondle each other. Our love making began. Whenever we made love we totally gave to each other.

Nothing else mattered at that time; only total satisfaction for each of us. Our loving temporarily relieved my mind from the strange happening that plagued me.

We had recently completed our training in pure sensitivity, and our love making had been enhanced by it beyond description. We now had learned to merge our bodies and minds.
It was truly a beautiful experience.

Slowly our minds and bodies turned from our high. Unfortunately, we were both still faced with our initial problem. First, we had to decide what we were going to do about it. After some brief discussion, we decided we would have to forego our schooling for a period of time and get to the bottom of this once and for all. We got dressed and we went to our mentor at the School. We asked for permission to discontinue our studies for a short period of time. We knew we would be granted permission since, whenever we had asked for permission in the past for time away from our studies, we never encountered a problem. It wasn't a question of going somewhere else to find the answers. We decided to stay on campus at my place. Marion moved some of her things into my place, and that first evening we decided not to delay but to get right to it.

We both sat facing each other. I tried to clear my mind. We sat like this for hours. I really have to admire Marian because, just on the strength of my word, she had gone along with this. I'm not sure I would have done the same. We tried this off and on all day long. When I would try to give up, Marian would push me into continuing just a little longer. By the time evening arrived, all we had to show for our time was sore limbs and extremely tired minds.

I believe Marian was trying as hard as I was. She didn't even know what she was looking for. We'd both had the same training for meditation. When we started looking for something through meditation, we usually came up with the same answers or conclusions. This was the first time either of us had ever drawn a blank in our meditation exercises. We had always come up with solutions to problems or found inventive new ideas. Today we were at a loss to understand what was happening. By the end of the day, between the despair of not finding answers to my transition to invisibility and our earlier serious lovemaking, we were both very tired. When we decided to go to bed, we just kissed goodnight and tried to get some sleep.

I had nearly drifted off to sleep when I was suddenly awakened by a predominant tone which suddenly crashed into my mind as if it were a collision. I quickly sat up in bed and gave Marian a nudge to awaken her. She turned over toward me. One look at the smile on my face, and she instinctively knew what had happened. She asked me to tell her what it sounded like. I told her to get her music-maker, and see if she could duplicate the sound for me. She quickly got it and began running the tones up and down the scale, searching for a sound to compare with the sound in my head. I told her that none of them even came close. They probably were basic tones, and I believed the tone I was hearing was likely a harmonic of the basic tones. I said that I was going to try and manipulate the tone again. I asked her to watch me and see if I dissolved before her eyes. Within a moment I had ran the tone up to the proper level. From the look on Marian's face, I knew that I had disappeared before her eyes. She nearly fainted! I knew that she was shocked; even though earlier she appeared to have accepted the reality of it. I realized that her earlier acceptance was merely for my benefit. This time she was genuinely aware of the seriousness of the matter.

I decided to experiment for a moment. I immediately pictured the craggy mountains of the Western Hemisphere and found myself atop one of its highest peaks. I felt no cold from the wind, though I knew it should have been there. A shadow of fear crossed my mind and I wondered if I would be able to return. I knew that at this moment I must be at least 300,000 cylinders from my quad. Immediately I thought of my quad and Marian. I found myself back in my quad. Marian was running through my quad, calling my name frantically. I ran to her and threw my arms around her. My body slowly materialized. She collapsed in my arms. She began to cry. I carried her to our bed and cuddled her in my arms until we both fell fast asleep. I wanted to wait until morning to tell her of my experiment in the Western Hemisphere.

Chapter IV

Keeping Secret's

I woke the next morning with the tone in my head. I was quite surprised, until I realized that it had always been there and I had just overlooked it. How could I have overlooked it? It had always been in my subconscious mind. I suspected that, perhaps, we all have it. We just suppress it.

Marian woke up a few minutes later, and I told her about the tone. She admitted that, from time to time in her life, there had been a tone sound in her head. She said she had shrugged it off until it finally went away. I explained that the tone was the sound that I used to manipulate my body density. We got out of bed and I showed her how I could fade in and out. We sat for hours waiting for Marian to try and find her tone. We went into deep meditation.

It took almost all day for her to find a tone sound in her head. With some practice, she was able to manipulate the frequency. I suggested she increase the frequency to its highest degree and see what happened. She nodded and began. To my amazement she literally disappeared before my eyes. A few minutes later she reappeared, and she was smiling the biggest smile I had ever seen on her lovely face. We both embraced and danced around the room with excitement.

We decided to try manipulating the mind tones together. We faced one another and began. Within a few moments, I knew she had disappeared, and I felt she was behind me. Mentally, I called to her, and, in my mind, I heard her reply. She was laughing impishly. She said she could see me but not too clearly. When I cleaned my mind of other thoughts, I began to make out the outline of her nude body. It was perfect. I couldn't help smiling when I realized she, too, was seeing my nude frame. It was as it should be. I took her by the hand and, telepathically asked, "Where to, Madame?" For the next hour or so we bounced across our planet like a bouncing ball. Stopping here and there for a moment and, then going places; places we hadn't had time to see in our normal life.

Finally we decided to return to my quad. Instantly we were both there and returned to our normal flesh bodies.

We were both overly tired from the strain. We had changed from flesh body to invisible body nearly a hundred times this day and traveled who knows how many cylinders distance. We both fell asleep exhausted.

The next morning I had a flash of insight. Of course it all became clear to me. Even gods must evolve. Evolution is a natural thing. Sooner or later, we all would evolve into something no one could imagine. We all know that. Every once in an eon a new specie appears with that one extra ingredient that begins the new strain. Perhaps Marian and I are the beginning of that new breed. How wonderful, I thought. Then it came to me. For eons of time all those who have heralded in a new era have been, at the time, despised by their fellow man, and were either killed, ridiculed or went into exile. I thought, if that is the case, Marian and I would have nothing to worry about. We would just keep this as our little secret. We wouldn't tell anyone about our "new ability".

When Marian woke up I brought breakfast to her in bed. There was a radiance about her that always followed a good love making session. After she had finished her breakfast, I told her of my latest intuition. She thought it over carefully and finally said she tended to agree with me. We were probably a newly evolved strain. We agreed to keep this a secret between us and not tell a soul. We would just use this new ability for our own personal pleasure as discreetly as possible.

Chapter V

Graduation

We began our studies again. We continued without incident, for nearly two years. One day, while we were in class, our instructor was lecturing in a monotone voice about some boring subject. I listlessly let my mind wander. Suddenly the tone came on into my mind unconsciously. I shifted the tone and vanished before the instructor's eyes. Marian nearly choked when she saw me disappear. The instructor broke the pointer he had been flourishing before the class. I was brought back with a start, knowing what a fool I'd been to allow myself to disappear in class. Marian and I well knew that this was bound to happen sooner or later. We simply refused to admit to ourselves that it could happen so spontaneously. The instructor began barking questions at me: how I did that, where did I learn this, and so forth. I merely pretended I didn't know who he was talking to. I tried to convince him, in vain, that I didn't know what he was talking about. It was no use. He refused to ignore it happening. I finally told him that this had happened to me occasionally but that I had no control over it. He requested that I be at the High System House the next morning to answer to the Master of the School. He also told me to bring Marian with me.

That evening Marian and I decided to have a good meal. Then we were going to transport ourselves all around the planet before bedtime and have a good love making session before retiring for the night. We had put our troubles behind us, and enjoyed a wonderful night.

Early the next morning we both appeared before the Master of the School, we had no idea what to expect. The Master solemnly told us to enter his quarters. He commanded us to be seated opposite him. He began. "My children, thousands of years ago this same incident occurred where the male and female counterpart of the species began to display vanishing tendencies. The Master, in those days, was well aware of what was happening; I too am clearly aware. This is, as you must know, not indicative of a new strain for our species. However, it is a strain which we as gods feel we could do better without. We have, as our sole transportation on this planet, our "teleporters" which serve us well. For all other needs such as food, shelter, and weather, we've created what we need with the powers inherent in us. Now, this new power that you've exposed to us is, in fact, not new to the "Masters", but ancient. I must tell you that it has, in all cases, caused more headaches for those who express the ability to do this than they ever imagined. In the past, those who have come up with this strain have been dealt with in the same way. Knowing that you've both nearly mastered your god abilities, in school and that the remaining years of your training would

24

be merely practice, I have decided to cut your schooling short. This would be of no harm to either of you. The Masters of this School have gathered during the early hours this morning. We have created for you, on the other end of the Galaxies, a group of planets in the normal atomic structure. I will teleport you, Adrian and Marian, this day to one of the planets to begin your own work as gods."

With a wave of his hand, we both vanished. It was then that I appeared here in the freezing weather; weather where my body is slowly becoming frozen. I now see before me the image of my lovely Marian. Using the power deep within the recesses of my mind, I changed the frozen surroundings to a lush green meadow, enhanced with every imaginable fruit tree. Marian and I thus will begin our life's journey together in this paradise that we call "Earth".

The End.

ISBN 978-0-578-03445-4

www.ingramcontent.com/pod-product-compliance
Lightning Source LLC
Chambersburg PA
CBHW071231130626
46555CB00004B/1932